DELL 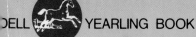 YEARLING BOOK

44437 •1.50

Three fourth, graders are
up to their usual antics at St. Anthony's School.

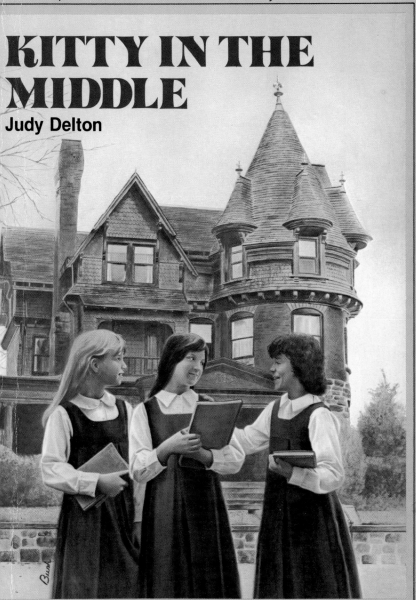

KITTY IN THE MIDDLE

Judy Delton

C.

KITTY

IN THE MIDDLE

KITTY
IN THE MIDDLE

Judy Delton

Illustrated by Charles Robinson

A YEARLING BOOK

Published by
Dell Publishing Co., Inc.
1 Dag Hammarskjold Plaza
New York, New York 10017

For Shirley,
As a Substitute Chevrolet

Yearling ® TM 913705, Dell Publishing Co., Inc.

ISBN: 0-440-44437-3

Reprinted by arrangement with Houghton Mifflin Company
Printed in the United States of America
First Yearling printing—September 1980
CW

For Shirley,
As a Substitute Chevrolet

Contents

1

The First Day of School

Kitty and Margaret Mary and Eileen had been friends since first grade. Actually, it was more that Kitty was a friend of Eileen's, and Margaret Mary was a friend of Kitty's. So sometimes they all played together, and sometimes Kitty played with Eileen alone and sometimes with Margaret Mary alone. Margaret Mary was safe and Eileen was dangerous and Kitty was somewhat of a chameleon, taking on the personality of whichever one she was with.

The girls went to Saint Anthony's Parochial School together. The new school year was about to begin, and they would be going into the fourth grade. Kitty didn't care for school, even though she would be glad to see her friends again after the long summer vacation. She lived five blocks from Saint Anthony's on Jefferson Avenue in a small white bungalow next to Stenstrom's Grocery and Meat Market. She was an only child, and Mrs. Thone, who lived next door, once said that Kitty was S-P-O-I-L-E-D (she spelled it out), but Kitty knew very well what the word meant, and disagreed.

Every morning Kitty's father took the streetcar to Minneapolis to work at the telephone company, and every evening at 5:30 when he came home, Kitty's mother had dinner waiting as he came up the steps. On Monday they had breaded veal and on Wednesday they had pork chops, and on Friday they had tuna. If it was Lent they had tuna every day.

On cold winter evenings, Kitty and her father went on walks together and could see, through the windows of the houses that they passed, people all warm and cozy, listening to the war news on their radios. Ever since before last Christmas, in 1941 when the Japanese bombed Pearl Harbor, people listened to the radio a lot. Kitty remembered the day that the war started because they had just come home from Norwood where her Aunt Katie lived, and everyone was so alarmed that Kitty went to bed and cried because she thought that meant there would be no Christmas, and she had looked forward to it all year.

Her best friend, Margaret Mary, lived on Saint Clair Avenue, which was four blocks farther from Saint Anthony's than Kitty's house, so she didn't have to go home at noon and could bring her lunch in a brown paper bag. Father Bauer had said that a pupil must live at least eight blocks from school to stay for lunch, and Margaret Mary lived nine blocks away in an old house with two staircases and a piano with framed photographs lining the top of it. She had three sisters and a brother. Every night her mother or one of her sisters would set her hair in rags, and every morning Margaret Mary would have long, perfect sausage curls. Her uniform was the only one at Saint Anthony's that was homemade, but it didn't matter because she always looked neat and clean.

Everything about Margaret Mary matched. She was just right. Even though her blouse collars were round instead of pointed like the regulation collars, no one said anything or called her names like they did Delores Henley, who also had homemade blouses. People liked Margaret Mary. She was honest and fair and got all A's in school. When Father Bauer came to the classroom every six weeks to pass out report cards and sing the marks out loud, the song for Margaret Mary was always the same. "An A and an A and an A-plus and an A," he would sing like an auctioneer, and Margaret Mary would walk up the aisle and say, "Thank you, Father," and walk back to her seat with her eyes down. She wasn't a showoff. She acted as though it would be just as well if she got all C's. But everyone, including Father Bauer, knew she never would.

Eileen, who was Kitty's other best friend, was also an only child and lived in a house with a fireplace and bookshelves lining the living room wall. She had a room of her own with furniture that matched. Her dressing table had an organdy skirt and her bed had a fat comforter, satin and smooth, folded in a triangle at the foot.

Eileen always wanted to be older than she was and change her name to Dorothy and travel around the world alone. She could lie very easily and smile at the same time and it didn't bother her that she would go to hell and burn forever for doing that.

Eileen lived on Juno Street, which was in the opposite direction from the way Kitty and Margaret Mary walked. It was only one block from school, but across an open field, and Eileen said that if you measured, it was really equal to eight city blocks and so it wasn't fair to say that she lived just one block from school, especially in winter when the wind swept across the snow-covered field and, with no houses to protect her, blew up a sharp Minnesota chill. The girls agreed that it seemed unfair that Eileen couldn't bring her lunch in a brown paper bag and had to go back and forth four times a day, when that one block was really eight. But rules were rules and the principal, Sister Justina, said, "What's good for Peter is good for Paul. What's good for one is good for all."

Halfway between Kitty's house and Eileen's house, and a block from school, was a large old three-story house with peeling paint and red brick turrets on the top. Crumbling steps led from the sidewalk to a long, overgrown path that wound its way to the front door. It was rumored that the city had condemned the house but that the people who lived there wouldn't move. Others said someone had been murdered there. Kitty had heard that it used to be an orphanage and that bad children were still held captive in the red turrets and were starving, but Margaret Mary said that it was just an old house, because she didn't spread rumors or listen to gossip. Eileen, on the other hand, knew for a fact that it was haunted.

But whatever its history, they often wondered who lived there and dreamed of finding a way to see the inside. When Kitty went to Eileen's house after school and Eileen walked her halfway home afterward, the old house was their parting point. They would stand and gaze up at the third floor and shiver.

"It's a dungeon, and it's haunted," Eileen would say. Kitty thought that now that they were beginning the fourth grade, maybe they'd be brave enough to find out. And whether she was ready to start school or not, Labor Day drew near and the day after, Saint Anthony's opened. The only good thing Kitty could see about it was that she would have new shoes, and they were not brown oxfords.

Just before Labor Day Kitty had called Margaret Mary on the phone.

"You should see them," she said to Margaret Mary. "They are in the Emporium window. They're called huaraches, and they are really hep."

"My mother said that the only kind of shoes for school are oxfords. They're serviceable and good for your feet, too."

"I know," said Kitty. "That's what my

8

mother says, too, but I hate oxfords."

After the girls had hung up, Kitty pleaded with her mother to take her shopping. When she pointed out the huaraches in the store window, her mother said, "Those are summer shoes. You would be able to wear them only through September and October. You'll need winter shoes in November."

"I'll wear them all year," cried Kitty, "winter and summer. I've got my birthday money — please, Mom?"

"It's not just the money, it's the ration stamps. Our shoe ration coupons would be gone for the year."

"You said Auntie Jo didn't need hers."

Kitty's mother considered that for a moment. "We'll see," she said finally. "If Jo has some extra, we'll think about it."

"We'll think about it," always meant yes to Kitty. Her Auntie Jo had closets full of shoes. "Where did Auntie Jo ever get all the ration coupons for those shoes?" Kitty had once asked her mother.

"She got them before shoes were rationed, and you didn't need coupons," her mother had said.

"You mean, once you could buy all the shoes you wanted?"

"Of course," said Kitty's mother. "After the war is over, we probably will again. And all the meat we want, and nylons, and gasoline." Kitty could not imagine a time when people did not have to stand in long lines with ration coupons to buy almost everything. It was as hard to believe as finding out that President Roosevelt hadn't always been president.

"Sure," said Kitty's Auntie Jo the next day when her mother asked if she had extra shoe stamps. So Kitty gave her mother her gift money and they went to the Emporium and bought the huaraches. They were woven from thin straps of leather and had open toes and open heels, and they squeaked when Kitty walked. She held them tightly all the way home, and put them on as soon as she got there. Later, she hated to take them off when she went to bed.

The next morning was the first day of school. Kitty met Margaret Mary at the corner. "I-yay ave-hay ot-gay y-may ew-nay oes-shay on-yay!" said Kitty excitedly in pig Latin. In third grade, they had loved to talk pig Latin, and every now and then they still did, even though they felt they were too old for it. They talked pig Latin by putting the last sound of a word first, and the first sound last with "ay" on the end.

"Ice-nay," said Margaret Mary. She was wearing new sturdy brown oxfords that were stiff and shiny and would last all year. "Ay-they eak-squay," she said.

"I know it," said Kitty. "All huaraches squeak."

The girls walked along, waving to the children they knew as they came out of their

11

houses. They all had clean faces and combed hair and new notebooks, and crayons that still had paper wrapped around them and pointed tips. Even though Kitty wasn't glad to see school start, she was caught up in the feeling of beginnings, and she felt especially proud to be wearing new shoes that were not like what everyone else was wearing. When they saw Eileen coming across the field, they waved and ran to catch up with her. She was wearing her black patent leather Mary Janes with the buckle in the middle. Kitty had Mary Janes, too, but she could only wear them on Sundays and on days when she went downtown to the Golden Rule for lunch.

"You've got huaraches!" said Eileen. "Nice."

Kitty was pleased that she had noticed. The girls got into line to go to church. Every opening day, Father Bauer had a mass for the whole school in which he asked

God's blessing on the new school year and prayed for the health of the students and teachers. The boys wore dark pants and light shirts and any belt that would not scratch the pews and desks, but the girls were all dressed alike in navy uniforms and white blouses. Kitty never thought it fair that the boys didn't have to wear uniforms. The girls wore chapel veils pinned to their hair, except for Eileen, who had forgotten hers and was wearing a Kleenex on her head. Sister Ursuline noticed and glared at her. The rule that said girls must have their heads covered in church did not mean Kleenex, Sister said with her eyes.

"I-yay ate-hay er-hay," whispered Kitty to Eileen.

"E-shay is-yay oing-gay o-tay e-bay our-yay eacher-tay is-thay ear-yay," Eileen whispered back. Kitty nodded her head. She had known that Sister Ursuline would be their teacher this year, and there was no way of escaping her unless they moved away or she died during the summer. And she hadn't. They could see that.

"I hear she tied Maurice Manderfeld to his seat last year," whispered Kitty to Eileen.

"I know she hit him over the head with her music pointer. She's mean."

Father Bauer was singing the Gloria now, when suddenly it happened. Sister Ursuline bent down to pick up a holy card that had fallen from her prayer book onto the kneeler, and her veil swept to the floor for a moment. A moment was all that Gerald Calder needed. He was standing next to Sister Ursuline as a disciplinary measure, and when he saw her veil on the floor, he quickly planted his foot squarely on the black serge, then looked the other way. He appeared to be studying his missal avidly, turning pages and moving ribbons to find the exact spot in the Gloria that Father Bauer was on.

Sister Ursuline tried to lift her head. She

14

couldn't. She tried again. There was a slight ripping sound. Gerald studied his missal closer. "Gerald!" hissed Sister Ursuline from the depths of the pew. Gerald continued to read, watching Father Bauer and mouthing the Latin along with the altar boys.

The boys and girls nearby would have laughed if they hadn't been so stunned that Gerald Calder could have such courage. To step on a nun's veil was the bravest thing anyone could dream of. No one had counted on something this exciting happening on the first day of school.

"Gerald!" hissed Sister again, rapping his foot sharply with her knuckle. "Move your foot this instant!" Gerald read on.

"He'll be expelled," whispered Kitty.

"He wants to go to the public school anyway," Eileen answered.

Kitty watched in horror. Gerald would surely be going to the public school. Why,

Henry Lees had been expelled for carving his desk with his penknife last year, and this was much worse than that.

The girls watched Sister Ursuline tugging away. "She deserves it," said Eileen without sympathy. "She's a witch."

Margaret Mary stared at Eileen. "You're supposed to respect anyone who wears the habit," she whispered.

Margaret Mary looked as though she might go to Sister Ursuline's rescue. But what could she do? Push Gerald Calder over? She might pull Sister's headpiece off in her efforts and Sisters had no hair, it was said. That would be even worse. Kitty hoped Margaret Mary wouldn't help Sister Ursuline.

Sister's headdress was already sliding to one side as she tried to get up. She appeared to be choking and gasping for air. Kitty wondered if it was from the headdress caught under her neck, or from shock. She had heard that old people could die from deep emotional strain.

"Gerald!" shouted Sister, in tones that everyone, including Gerald, could not avoid hearing. "You are standing on my veil! Move your foot immediately!" Sister Ursuline did not sound as though she were dying. Gerald looked to the side in great surprise, then looked down as if absolutely shocked.

"Excuse me, Sister," he said, moving his foot and freeing the trapped veil at last. "I had no idea."

Sister stood up slowly and adjusted her headpiece while she tried to regain her composure. Her face was very red, and Gerald looked apologetic. "I'm so sorry," he murmured. Maybe he won't get expelled, thought Kitty. Sister closed her lips together tightly. "We'll discuss it after mass," she said.

"*Ite missa est!*" sang Father Bauer, turning

toward the students for the first time and lifting his arms up in great sweeping motions. His red vestments hung to the floor and draped from his arms like giant, elaborate bats' wings, and the altar boys answered, *"Deo gratias."*

Sister's face was still red and her lips tightly closed as she herded the children out of church. She glared at Eileen's Kleenex again and frowned at the squeak of Kitty's shoes. Once outside, Gerald was sent to Father Bauer's office, but nothing more was said about the veil incident. Sister seemed anxious to forget it, or maybe pretend that it hadn't happened at all.

The students went to their new rooms, and as soon as they were all settled in, Sister Ursuline said, "The first thing we will do today is to assign study partners for the library." This was one of the most exciting parts of the first day of school. Each student spent an hour every day in the library with a partner, and it could be all fun and private jokes, and the time could go fast. Or, if your partner was someone you didn't like, it could be awful — then time would drag.

"I hope I get to be with you or Eileen," said Kitty to Margaret Mary. Margaret Mary hoped so too, although she would get along with whoever her partner was. She always did. Still, she would rather be with Kitty.

Eileen really didn't care whom she had for a partner. She liked to sit by herself and read books about faraway countries, and it didn't much matter what her partner was doing.

But it was very important to Kitty that she be with a friend. She crossed her fingers because she knew that very often Sister Ursuline purposely put people together who weren't friends. Eileen could be right, she thought. Maybe Sister Ursuline was a witch.

Sister began to call off the partners. "Thomas Kelly and Virgil Bliss," she called. They came to the front and stood together, Thomas frowning and Virgil smiling. Then Sister called Margaret Mary and Eileen, and they walked to the front of the room.

"Darn!" said Kitty. Now she was worried.

"Kitty and Delores," called Sister.

Kitty's stomach ached. Delores Henley, whose nose was always running and who had homemade blouses with round collars and stains down the front of her wrinkled uniform. Delores with the flat, plain face. Of all people Kitty hated to be near.

Kitty walked to the front of the room, her huaraches going *squeak squeak* all the way. At least everyone would see her new shoes, there was that to be thankful for, anyway. She was glad they squeaked. No one could help but notice them. Kitty got to the front of the room and stood still, but she could still hear a squeaking noise behind her. The noise stopped when it got to her side. Kitty looked down. She couldn't believe her eyes. There beside her, on the feet of Delores Henley, were huaraches exactly like hers. Delores stood close beside Kitty, glad to be her library partner.

Kitty wished she were dead. She wanted to take the shoes off and throw them out the window. She wanted to take them back to the Emporium and get her money and Auntie Jo's ration stamps back. But it was too late. She had worn them, and they had tar on the soles, and anyway, the whole class had already seen that she and Delores Henley had shoes that were alike. Sure enough, Eileen was right. Sister Ursuline was indeed a witch. What Gerald had done served her right.

2

The Real Live Paper Dolls

Some afternoons after school Margaret Mary turned off on Jefferson Avenue with Kitty instead of going home, and they played together until suppertime. They usually played at Kitty's instead of Margaret Mary's because it was easier; Margaret Mary didn't have to change her uniform or let her mother know where she was. It wasn't that Margaret Mary's mother didn't care about her, it was just that she had more children than Kitty's mother did, and Margaret Mary was more responsible. Her mother knew she would be home at suppertime, and that she wouldn't get her uniform dirty if she played in it.

One afternoon they sat on Kitty's front porch playing with paper dolls. They kept them in candy boxes after they were cut out of the paper doll books, and in between the sets they put tissue paper. Movie stars were kept in one box, and baby dolls in another — that was the box they liked best and played with most. Only one doll came in the baby doll books and she was a whole page tall.

"I'm really tired of the same old dolls," said Kitty, looking at a row of them lined up along the wall of the porch. (They had to play there or the dolls and clothes would blow away.)

"There are no new ones at the dime store," said Margaret Mary. "We've got them all."

"I didn't mean that," said Kitty. "I'm tired of all of them. Let's make our own."

"We've done that before, their clothes never fit right," said Margaret Mary.

Kitty thought about that. "I mean make some that are so different no one ever saw any like them." She squinted. "How could we make them so different that everyone would wish they were us? If you could have any paper doll you wanted, what would it be like?"

Margaret Mary thought awhile. "I know one thing," she said. "It would be huge, just huge."

Kitty snapped her fingers. "That's it!" she said. "Let's make paper dolls as big as we are!"

"Ha," said Margaret Mary. "Even the butcher wouldn't give us enough paper for that."

Kitty frowned. "Butcher paper wouldn't be heavy enough anyway. We need something stiff, but wood would be too hard to cut."

The girls stared out the porch windows at the traffic going by. They could see people entering and leaving Stenstrom's grocery store next door. Just then the grocery door opened and Mr. Stenstrom set a large box outside. It had IVORY SNOW written in large letters on one side.

"Kitty!" shouted Margaret Mary. "I've got an idea. Come on!"

Kitty followed Margaret Mary across the porch floor strewn with paper dolls. They went out the front door and around the lilac hedge that ran between Kitty's house and the store. "See that box?" said Margaret Mary. "What does Mr. Stenstrom do with the boxes that the soap and cereal come in?"

"He burns them in the back yard every night," answered Kitty.

"Swell!" said Margaret Mary. "Then he doesn't want them! Kitty, do you know how big a cardboard carton is when it is opened up and cut down the sides? We can make life-size dolls with them!"

"That's what I meant!" said Kitty. "Dolls

that are different from what anyone else has!"

"These will be," Margaret Mary promised.

The girls walked into the grocery store to ask Mr. Stenstrom if he was getting rid of the box in front of the store. "I burn it tonight," he said cheerfully. "More in the back, if you want them." The girls shouted thank you and raced to the storeroom.

"Wow!" said Kitty. "There are lots! Let's take the biggest ones there are."

The girls lifted box after box, looking for just the right ones. Ones without too much writing on them, ones that were high and wide and not bent or dirty. Pretty soon they had more than they could carry.

"Let's cut them on the back lawn," said Kitty, thinking of what her mother would say if they brought them into the house. "I'll get scissors and crayons and stuff."

When she came back, they cut the boxes

carefully down their seams, so that they were flat. "Now!" said Margaret Mary. "Lie down on this box and I'll trace you."

Kitty lay down flat and Margaret Mary traced around her with a black crayon. Then they cut open another box and Kitty traced around Margaret Mary. They set to work cutting them out.

"This is hard, cutting through cardboard," said Kitty, with her tongue between her teeth. Margaret Mary didn't seem to be having as much trouble. Her scissors just moved right along and the doll looked neat, just like Margaret Mary.

When Kitty was through cutting she decided to go around her doll again in places. There didn't seem to be any reason why she couldn't have a thin doll, thinner than Margaret Mary's. The edges were a little jagged and she would just even them off.

"Look!" said Margaret Mary. "The knees and hips bend just where the box was folded. My doll can kneel and sit and stand."

Kitty looked. Her own doll bent at the chest and in the middle of the legs. Maybe coloring would help. The girls laid their dolls out flat and began to color them carefully.

"What color dress are you going to have?" asked Kitty.

"Blue," said Margaret Mary. "Blue is my favorite color, for the Blessed Virgin Mary."

"That's what I was going to use," said Kitty.

"Well, they shouldn't be alike. With only two dolls, they should look different from each other. I'll use pink if you want blue."

"Okay," said Kitty, and began to color. The girls colored all afternoon. They put saddle shoes on the dolls, and white anklets and angora sweaters. Margaret Mary's doll had long curls like hers, and a locket around her neck. Kitty's had a silver choker, but when she held it up, the doll looked as though she had a large bandage around her neck.

"There!" said Margaret Mary. "She's done! What do you think?"

Kitty looked at the doll. It looked just like Margaret Mary. Neat and beautiful with a round blouse collar over her sweater and sleeves that were the right length.

"It's like having a sister," said Margaret Mary. "She's big enough to be real. Let's pretend they are really our sisters. And we get along real well and we do everything with them. Maybe we can make husbands for them when they grow up, and children and even houses out of boxes for them to live in, with beds and tables and chairs. And cars," she said. "Even cars!"

Margaret Mary's words made Kitty's head spin with possibilities. There was only one thing the matter, she thought to herself, her doll was not pretty. It was too thin and had

a bandage around the neck and the legs seemed too long and the body too short and the head too small.

"Margaret Mary?"

"Ummm?" said Margaret Mary, putting a charm bracelet on her doll's wrist.

"I like your doll better than mine."

"So do I," said Margaret Mary.

"Will you make me one just like yours?"

"Of course not," said Margaret Mary. "We can't have the same kind."

"Well, will you make me one just as nice only different? I'll give you two V-Mail letters from my cousin."

"I've got a V-mail letter. From my uncle."

Kitty thought again. She knew something Margaret Mary would really like. Before she could regret it she blurted out, "My little silver rosary in the silver box with the velvet in it. I'll give it to you."

Margaret Mary looked surprised. She

liked Kitty's rosary. It was not like any other she had ever seen, and now she could have it just for making a paper doll.

Kitty didn't want to take time to think about what her mother might say. She ran into the house and came out with the rosary. "Here," she said.

Margaret Mary took the little silver box. She opened it and saw the rosary shining on the blue velvet. "Are you sure?" she asked.

Kitty nodded her head.

"Well, thank you," said Margaret Mary, putting the rosary in her blouse pocket.

"Let's cut this and I'll make you a new doll," she said reaching for another box.

Margaret Mary made Kitty a doll that was almost like her own. She put a wristwatch on her arm and flowers in her hair. The arms and legs bent in the right place and nothing was too long or too short. It was very nice, but not as nice as hers. Which was only fair, she explained. If she made it for herself, she would have made it extraspecial, but it was certainly a better-looking doll than Kitty's first one.

"I love it!" said Kitty.

They pretended that the dolls were their sisters. Then they pretended that they were their mothers. After supper they pretended they were Red Cross nurses and USO hostesses. Then they were English war brides and ladies whose husbands went off to war and never returned. These dolls cried a lot. There was no doubt about it, it was fun playing with life-size paper dolls.

But as the day wore on into early evening, Kitty began to think about her rosary. The crayon was beginning to smear and the doll felt damp and Kitty wondered if cardboard could last forever. She knew the silver rosary would.

"I'm tired of these dolls," she said.

Margaret Mary looked surprised. "We can play tomorrow."

Kitty shook her head. "The dolls are

wearing out. Look how soggy they are."

Margaret Mary looked at the dolls. They did look a little worn. Then she thought of the rosary in the silver box in her pocket. It didn't seem right somehow to take a rosary for doing something for a friend. Especially an expensive silver rosary. It might even be stealing . . .

With sudden decision, she reached into her blouse pocket. "Kitty?" she said. "I'll take the V-Mail letters instead of the rosary for making the doll."

"Really?" said Kitty, looking up. "But you already have a V-Mail letter."

"I think I'll collect them."

Kitty ran to her room to get the letters and put the rosary safely away. When she returned the girls brought the dolls into the house. Then they cleaned up the scraps in the yard.

"You know these dolls might dry out and we can play tomorrow," said Kitty.

"Sure they will," said Margaret Mary.

35

"They'll be dry, and I'll bet we could make clothes for them out of some old dresses."

"I've got some old hats in the attic that would fit," said Kitty.

"Good! See you tomorrow," said Margaret Mary, waving as she rode off on her bike toward home.

3

Kitty's Bad Habit

The days at Saint Anthony's school were pretty much alike, but every once in a while something happened that was different. On a morning after the real paper dolls were forgotten, Sister Ursuline took attendance as usual and collected milk money. Then the children said their morning prayers and an extra prayer to Saint Damian, who was the saint for the day. After they had all saluted the flag and sat down, Sister Ursuline asked them to please stand up and sit down again three times without banging their desks. Everyone was ready for her to say, "Take out your geography books, children," but instead she said,

"This morning we are going to talk about bad habits."

Kitty looked around at Margaret Mary and smiled. Any change in routine was welcome. Then she looked at Eileen, who sat in front. Eileen had her hands folded in the middle of her desk and was looking up at Sister Ursuline as though she were very interested in bad habits.

"I think," said Sister Ursuline, "that now, just before Advent, is a good time to think about bad habits." She lifted her veil over her shoulder. It would be nice to be a nun, Kitty thought, and have a swishy veil and long dress, even if it was black, and have everyone get up when you came into a room and say, "Good morning, Sister," all together, and order boys and girls around, and have them do whatever you said. Kitty could smell the serge as Sister swept up the aisle past her. Some of the children reached out and touched Sister's veil as she passed by them, and sometimes the rosary that was around her waist caught on a desk or inkwell. It was unexpected things like these that made the day eventful.

Sister was in front of the room again, in front of Eileen's desk. "Everyone has a bad habit. Everyone here does something that he or she is not proud of and should work to overcome." They all glanced around the room, thinking of each other's bad habits.

"I want you to close your eyes for five minutes and think of one of your bad habits that is worse than any other. I will ask you to tell that bad habit to the class. Then we will work for a whole week to overcome that habit, and in a week I will check on the progress everyone has made."

It was quiet in the room as everyone began thinking of bad habits. Kitty looked around. Several of her classmates were waving their hands in the air. They were anxious to be the first to tell their bad habit. Kitty was beginning to feel nervous. She thought and thought but couldn't remember any bad habit she had. After a while, she couldn't even *think* at all. Her mind seemed fuzzy and blank. The minutes ticked away on the clock in the front of the room and she watched the big hand slide down to the next dot. Every time it slid, it meant another minute was gone . . . Once Kitty had not come home from school right away; she had stopped at the candy store when her mother had told her not to. But that wasn't really a habit. A habit was something you did over and over again, like brushing your teeth.

"Time is up," said Sister Ursuline. "We will begin in front and go up and down the rows. Eileen, will you tell us your bad habit?"

"Yes, Sister," said Eileen, standing up beside her desk, shaking her short, bouncy curls, which were tied in a yellow satin ribbon today. "I never look before I cross the street. My mother says I should get into the habit of looking both ways."

"My, yes," said Sister Ursuline. "That is a bad habit, and dangerous. Why, if you don't change that bad habit, you could be hit by a passing car."

"I know," said Eileen, pleased that Sister was alarmed about her bad habit. Everyone nodded. That was a good bad habit. Eileen sat down.

Kitty thought to herself, I always look before I cross the street. That can't be my bad habit. Sister continued around the room, and her turn was coming closer and closer.

"I don't say my morning prayers," said Gerald Calder. "I'll bet he doesn't say *any* prayers," thought Kitty. She always said her morning prayers.

"I bite my fingernails," said Delores Henley. Everyone knew that because Delores always had her fingers in her mouth. Kitty didn't bite her fingernails.

It was Margaret Mary's turn. "I sometimes forget to put the cover back tightly on the peanut butter jar," she said. "My mother says the peanut butter could get rancid."

Kitty didn't forget to put covers back tightly on jars. She didn't put covers on at all because her mother made her sandwiches and got the meals and snacks and told Kitty not to touch the food.

Sister was moving on down the aisle. "Kitty?" she said. "Will you tell us your bad habit, please?" Kitty looked uncomfortable.

"I don't have a bad habit," she said.

Sister smiled. "Come, come, dear, we all have bad habits. Don't be afraid to speak up. We will work on it together, and by this time next week you will have improved."

Moments passed. The hand on the clock kept slipping down a dot and making a click. "We are waiting, Kitty," said Sister impatiently. Everyone was turning around and looking at Kitty.

"I bite my fingernails," said Kitty, her voice sounding loud in the quiet room.

"That is a bad habit, dear. You don't have to be ashamed to talk about it. You try hard to get over that habit this week."

Sister went on to the next person. Kitty felt hot and uncomfortable, but most of all she felt guilty. She didn't bite her finger-nails. Why had she said that? It was a lie, and she knew she shouldn't tell a lie even for a magnificent reason like saving all the souls in purgatory. And this was surely not as important as that. The more she thought about it, the worse she felt.

After they had all told their bad habits, the class had geography and spelling and reading. Later, at recess, Margaret Mary and Eileen came running up to Kitty on the playground. "I didn't know you bit your fingernails," said Eileen.

"I don't, said Kitty.

"Oh," said Eileen. "Let's play on the

teeter-totters today." She ran ahead to get the one on the end.

"You don't bite your fingernails," said Margaret Mary. "That was a lie."

"I know it," said Kitty. "I couldn't think. I don't think I have a bad habit."

"Well, you don't make them *up*. That's worse. Lying is a sin."

"I *know*," shouted Kitty.

All day Kitty couldn't think of anything else but the lie she had told. And the more she thought about it, the worse she felt. After school she said she didn't want to go to Eileen's house and play confession, and she didn't want to play dolls with Margaret Mary. She wanted to go home, alone.

When she got there, she went to her room and closed the door. She sat and thought some more until her mother called her for supper.

"Put the napkins on the table, Kitty," said her mother. "And wash your hands — here comes Daddy now."

44

As they ate, Kitty's father said, "What was new at school today?"

"Nothing."

"You are awfully quiet — are you coming down with a cold?" asked her mother. "Take your hands out of your mouth."

After supper Kitty's father helped her with her homework. He looked at her spelling paper. "Take your hands out of your mouth," he said.

Kitty's mother tucked her into bed at 8:30 and when she turned out the light, she said, "Why have you got your fingers in your mouth?"

"I'm biting my fingernails," said Kitty.

"You've never bitten your fingernails before," said her mother.

"I know," said Kitty, biting off the third one in a row. "I do now."

"That is a bad habit, you know. You will have to get over that."

"I'll try," said Kitty.

The next morning at the breakfast table,

Kitty was still biting her fingernails. "STOP THAT!" said her father.

Later, Kitty's mother took her father aside and said, "Kitty seems to have picked up the habit of biting her nails, Henry. I don't think we should shout at her, it will make it even worse. She will be more nervous. I have an idea . . ."

That afternoon when Kitty came home from school, her mother said, "Kitty, your father and I have discussed it, and if you stop biting your fingernails by the end of the week, we will buy you the birthstone ring you have been wanting."

"Really?" said Kitty.

"Do you think you can get over the habit?" said her mother.

"Yes," said Kitty, "I do."

Her mother looked relieved. "Well, try hard, I understand how hard it is to break a habit once it has taken hold," she said. Kitty's mother was very understanding.

That afternoon Kitty stopped biting her fingernails. It was not long before her mother and father noticed that she did not have her fingers in her mouth anymore. "I am pleased!" said her mother.

"If she lasts till Saturday, I'll believe she has it licked," said her father.

On Saturday Kitty's father came home with a small box, which he handed to her. "Daddy!" she shouted, opening it quickly. "What a beautiful ring! Thank you!" She gave her mother and father a kiss and a hug.

"You deserve it," they said. "Of course you have to stop biting your fingernails for good," said her mother.

"Of course," agreed Kitty.

On Monday morning after the flag salute and prayer and saint for the day, Sister Ursuline said, "Now! We will see how many people got over their bad habit this week.

Eileen, did you make any progress in watching for cars when you crossed the street?"

"No, Sister," said Eileen cheerfully.

"Well, habits are hard to break," said Sister kindly. "Some take lots of perseverance. You work on it again this week."

"Yes, Sister," said Eileen.

"Gerald, have you been saying your morning prayers?"

Gerald hung his head. "Well, sometimes, Sister."

"Sometimes is a good start," said Sister Ursuline. "We can't do it all at once."

"Delores, what about your fingernails? Have you stopped biting them?"

"Well, I tried Sister, but I can't seem to stop. My father says it is a big habit to break all at once."

"You will have to try harder, Delores. Can you try harder to break that habit this week?" said Sister, not seeming to heed the words of Delores' father.

"Yes, Sister," said Delores, who was red in the face and glad to have Sister move on to someone else.

Sister asked each of them about his or her habit. No one had stopped completely.

Then she came to Kitty. "Kitty, have you been able to control your fingernail biting?"

"Yes, Sister, I don't bite my fingernails anymore at all," said Kitty.

"Why!" said Sister Ursuline. "You have stopped completely?"

"Yes," said Kitty. "I have stopped for good. And I got this ring from my mother and father because I don't bite my fingernails anymore."

Kitty held up her hand for Sister to see. "It's my birthstone," she said. "And it's gold-plated."

"What a splendid example you are for all of us, Kitty! Come up and stand in front of the room so we can all clap!" Kitty walked up and stood beside Sister.

"Let this be an example to all of us. A bad habit can be broken. That is very inspiring, Kitty. Was it difficult to do?"

"No, Sister."

"Boys and girls, if Kitty can break this habit in a week, I am sure others can do the same."

At recess time everyone gathered around Kitty to see her ring.

"It doesn't seem fair," said Margaret Mary on the way home from school. "You just started to bite your fingernails."

"Yes it is," said Kitty. "I started. And I stopped. And that is one way to break a habit."

4

The Girls Attend a Wedding

The Minnesota winter grew colder and colder. Kitty bundled up in her teddy bear coat with the green down the front. (Eileen wore a red one, and when she walked Kitty halfway home they didn't linger at the old house that was their parting point).

Winter limited the girls' activities. After skating or sliding, they had to go to someone's house for the rest of the afternoon because it was too cold to be outside for very long at a time. One Saturday Kitty and Eileen and Margaret Mary were sitting in Kitty's bedroom, tired of playing Monopoly and Clue.

"I'd like to *do* something," said Kitty, who was always the most impatient one.

"Let's go look in the windows of the old house," said Eileen.

Margaret Mary looked at her. "That's spying," she said sternly.

"It sounds like fun," said Kitty, "but we might get caught. Anyway, it's too cold, we need to be inside where it's warm."

"There's a wedding at the church," said Margaret Mary, hoping to change the subject. "I love weddings, don't you?"

"Whose wedding is it?" asked Kitty.

"I don't know, but I saw the flower truck there this morning after mass." Margaret Mary went to mass with her parents every morning, even on Saturday.

"Well, we can't go to the wedding of people we don't know," said Kitty.

"Why not?" asked Eileen. "We would be doing them a favor by praying that they will be happy ever after."

Kitty and Margaret Mary thought about that. It made sense.

"I'll bet there's a reception in the basement of the church after the ceremony," said Eileen. "They'll have cake and sandwiches and ham and candy and nuts and stuff." She waved her hand. "All just there for anyone."

"Anyone?"

"Anyone who comes to the wedding." Eileen knew all about such things.

"That would be us!" said Kitty. "Let's go!"

The girls got into their ski pants first. Then they put on their warm coats and tassle caps and wrapped scarves around their necks.

"If you are going out, wear several pair of socks," called Kitty's mother.

The girls put on several pair of socks, then their snow boots. By the time they were ready to leave they could hardly move, but they didn't feel cold.

When they got to church they saw that Margaret Mary was right, there was a wedding — but it was half over. They stood in the back of the church and wondered what to do. "Maybe we should wait and go right to the reception," said Kitty.

"We can't go to the reception if we don't go to the wedding and pray for them," Margaret Mary insisted.

Just then an usher came up to the girls and asked whose side they'd be sitting on. Kitty and Margaret Mary wanted to run out the door and home. But Eileen just said, "The bride's," and walked behind the usher as he led the way. There was nothing the other two could do but follow.

People stared at them as they tracked snow up the white runner in the aisle. The organ was playing and a woman was singing "Ave Maria" in a very high voice. The girls genuflected, then rose from their knees and tumbled into a middle pew as quietly as possible, considering the snow boots.

"I like brides better than grooms," whispered Eileen. "They're prettier." Kitty and Margaret Mary nodded in agreement. They liked brides better too.

Flowers filled the church and bridesmaids with red velvet dresses and holly in their hair filled the front row. A woman in the third pew had tears in her eyes and was wiping her nose with a lacy handkerchief.

The girls watched while the bride and groom promised to love and cherish each other for better or worse until death did them part.

"Isn't that romantic," sighed Margaret Mary. "I'd like a wedding just like this some day."

"I like her dress," said Eileen.

Before long the organ began to play and the bride and groom turned around and started back down the aisle. They looked pink and happy, and were smiling and waving. Kitty and Margaret Mary and Eileen smiled and waved back. They noticed that the guests were beginning to leave the pews one by one and line up in the back of the church to kiss the bride and shake the groom's hand.

"Let's go out the side door," said Eileen, "and right down to the basement."

They were all the way down the stairs when Margaret Mary shouted, "I forgot to pray for them!"

"Pray at home," said Eileen.

"I can't eat their food if I don't pray for them in church," said Margaret Mary, turning around and heading back up again.

The girls trudged back up the stairs in their heavy, wet clothes behind Margaret Mary. They knelt down and waited for her to pray. By the time she was through, the line of guests in the back of the church had moved downstairs.

"I hope all the good stuff isn't gone," said Eileen. But she needn't have worried. There was lots and lots of food. "What are you going to have first?" she asked.

"Mints," said Kitty. "I love mints. And some of those fancy sandwiches that look like wedding bells."

The girls took plates and filled them, then carried them over to a card table set up in a corner. They unwrapped their scarves and opened their coats.

"This is good cake," said Eileen.

"I'm saving mine to take home and put under my pillow," said Margaret Mary. "You always put wedding cake under your pillow at night and it brings good luck. Maybe I'll have a rich, handsome husband some day."

Kitty looked at the cake with its red roses

and green leaves. "That sure must be messy in the morning when you get up!" she said.

"And it's dumb," said Eileen. "How could that possibly have anything to do with who your husband is going to be?"

"It does," said Margaret Mary firmly.

"Look," said Kitty. "They're taking pictures."

The girls watched a photographer take pictures of the bride cutting the cake and kissing the groom. As the bride was preparing to throw her bouquet, Eileen rose to get more food. She was walking by the table, when the large bouquet of roses with a white gardenia in the middle came hurtling toward her. The camera snapped just as she reached up and grabbed it. Everyone began to clap.

"Isn't she sweet!" said someone nearby.

"Probably a cousin of the groom's," someone added.

"I don't recognize her," murmured another voice.

Eileen smiled, showing her white teeth, and put the bouquet under her arm while she heaped more sandwiches on her plate. Then she walked back to the card table.

"Eileen! Do you know what? You're in their wedding picture!"

Eileen ate her cream cheese and nut sandwich.

"Look at that man," said Kitty. "He's coming over here."

Margaret Mary and Eileen looked. Sure enough, someone was heading for their table.

"I'll bet he's mad about the bouquet," said Kitty.

"And the picture," said Margaret Mary.

They sat speechless with fright and watched the man come closer. Eileen kept on eating.

When the man got to their table, he held

up a red mitten. "I wonder," he said, "if this belongs to one of you girls."

"Thank you," said Eileen. "It's mine." She reached out and took the mitten and put it in her coat pocket.

"Ah, are you friends of the bride and groom?" asked the man pleasantly.

Margaret Mary and Kitty turned bright red and looked at him with open mouths. They couldn't think of a thing to say. Kitty was afraid that Margaret Mary would tell the truth, but before either of them said a word, Eileen answered, "No, we're relatives."

"I see," said the man. "Well, you were lucky to catch the bouquet." He smiled as he moved on to another table of guests.

Kitty sighed with relief. Margaret Mary shouted under her breath, "Eileen, you lied! How can you lie, in the basement of a *church?*"

"I didn't lie," said Eileen.

"You said we were relatives!"

Eileen looked at Margaret Mary. "We are. We're brothers. Don't you believe Father Bauer?" she asked. "He said we are all brothers. All people are brothers. I've heard him say that."

Kitty and Margaret Mary thought about that. "But that's . . ."

"Aren't brothers relatives?" demanded Eileen. "Aren't they?"

Margaret Mary and Kitty thought some more. Father Bauer did say they all were brothers, and he wouldn't lie. And brothers surely were relatives.

Eileen picked up another sandwich.

"She's right, you know," said Kitty. "Father Bauer did say that."

But Margaret Mary still looked doubtful. Kitty quickly changed the subject.

"It's too bad your curls weren't showing. You had your cap on, and your curls would have been so nice in the picture."

Eileen shrugged.

"What a nice wedding," said Margaret Mary.

"Eileen will be in their photograph album forever," said Kitty. "I wonder who they are?"

The girls watched the people for a while, and when the bride and groom got ready to leave, they threw rice along with everyone else. Then it was time to go. "Wasn't that fun!" sighed Kitty.

As the girls buttoned their coats and tied their scarves, Eileen looked thoughtful. "I read in the church bulletin that there is a funeral at noon . . . They always have the funeral dinners down here in the basement afterward . . ."

Kitty and Margaret Mary looked aghast.

Eileen continued. "If we wait around a bit, we'll be just in time. We could go to the funeral and pray for his soul and then come down here for . . ."

Kitty and Margaret Mary put their mittens on. "It's time to go," said Margaret Mary. "Take your bouquet, Eileen. One reception for today is enough."

5

Valentine's Day

On one especially cold day when Kitty's mother insisted she wear a scarf over her face and one around her neck, besides her parka hood and teddy bear coat, she still had to run all the way down Jefferson Avenue to keep warm. At the corner where she met Margaret Mary every morning, it was hard to stand still and wait. Kitty shivered even with all the clothes she had on. There was frost on her scarf where she breathed and it felt stiff and cold, and she thought of the four more blocks they must walk after Margaret Mary came. Finally she saw her, running along with her brown

66

lunch bag in one hand and her book bag in the other. She had on her extrawarm coat, the one her mother had cut down and made over. Her mother always made over the larger coats that relatives had given them into ones for the children. She said, "There's a lot of wear still in that. The new wartime material is thin and sleazy and wouldn't keep a grasshopper warm."

It must have been true because Margaret Mary was never shivering like Kitty, although Kitty never could picture a cold grasshopper.

"There are two more gold stars on Berkley Street," said Margaret Mary. "That makes thirty-nine for me and twenty-six for you."

Gold stars in the house windows meant that the people living there had a serviceman who had been killed in action in the war. If there was a blue star, it meant someone in the family was in the service. The girls counted gold and blue stars just the way they counted cars with only one headlight. "Padiddle!" the one who saw a star first would shout. It was an ongoing game, and no one ever won; the girls just kept getting ahead of each other in turn. Eileen thought it was silly, but she played anyway.

"It's too cold to look for stars," said Kitty.

Margaret Mary didn't look cold. "We have to pray for their souls," she said. "It must be awful to have your brother or father killed in action. I always say, 'Eternal-rest-grant-unto-him-O-Lord. And-let-perpetual-light-shine-upon-him. May-he-rest-in-peace-amen,' whenever I see a gold star."

Kitty shook her head. "Sister Ursuline said to say that every time you hear an ambulance siren."

"Well, it's the same thing if someone dies in the war," said Margaret Mary. "Servicemen need prayers just as much as people dying around here."

"More," said Kitty, walking backward to keep the wind off her face. Kitty could never see any sense in saying that prayer when she heard an ambulance siren. Everyone in an ambulance was not necessarily dead. When Katie Blaske broke her leg, she was taken to the hospital in an ambulance, and she was far from dead. She probably wouldn't have liked to hear someone say that prayer for her. It might even make you dead if you weren't. It was possible, she imagined, for God to get mixed up. Margaret Mary's idea of saying the prayer for the gold stars made far more sense. Before the star went in the window the family was absolutely sure the person was dead, and most likely the funeral was even over.

The girls waited on the corner of Randolph for the patrol boys to put up the stop sign. The patrol boys had been told to wait until there were enough children on the corner to make stopping traffic worthwhile. Sometimes they did what they were supposed to do and sometimes they didn't. But this morning they were taking the rule seriously and were busy fencing with their stop signs while children watched on the corner. The girls jumped up and down on the curb, trying to keep warm. Finally a mother arrived with her kindergarten boy and waited in the car to see him cross the street. The patrol boys put up their signs and Kitty and Margaret Mary hurried across.

"What are all those kids doing by the fence?" said Kitty. "Just look at them."

As the girls got closer they could see someone in the middle of the crowd. He was a tall boy with wavy blond hair standing up high on his forehead like a movie star's, and he wasn't wearing a cap. In fact, he only had a suit coat on, and no winter jacket, either.

"I wonder who that is," said Margaret Mary. Now they could see that the crowd around him was mostly girls, and they were smiling and giggling. The new boy looked as if he was enjoying the attention immensely. The two girls saw Eileen coming along the sidewalk and waved.

"Who's that?" asked Kitty, motioning with her thumb.

Eileen looked. "Probably the new boy."

"What new boy?"

"I don't know. I heard someone say we were getting a new boy."

"In our room?"

"I guess so." The bell rang and everyone lined up. The new boy put out his arms as though he didn't know where to go. Immediately Ruthie Cobza said, "I'll show you where our room is, just walk with me." And he did. Everyone knew that Ruthie was boy crazy, and no one played with her.

When the girls got to their room and the

wraps were hung and prayers were said, Sister Ursuline announced, "Boys and girls, I want you to meet a new boy in our class." Sister took him by the arm. "This is Eugene Legget and he has just moved here from the South. He is from the state of Missouri. Eugene, you can take that desk next to the window." Sister gave him his books and everyone looked to see whom he sat by.

"Ruthie, since you sit near Eugene, would you show him where we are in arithmetic and help him if he has a question?"

"Yes, Sister," said Ruthie, going to Eugene's desk. He moved over, and Ruthie sat on the edge of his seat with an earnest look on her face and flipped the pages of his book.

At recess Ruthie got into line with Eugene and pointed out all of the items of interest, such as the bulletin board in the hall that said BUY WAR BONDS TODAY and "All for thee, O Sacred Heart of Jesus." Eugene looked at the bulletin board, and the wash-rooms, and the closet where the chalk and erasers were kept. Ruthie was doing an efficient job. On the playground, everyone gathered around Eugene again.

"Let's go to church and pray," said Eileen. Margaret Mary looked at her in surprise. In all the time she had known Eileen, never once had she volunteered to go to church.

"It's warmer," Eileen said.

Kitty glanced over at Eugene. She noticed that his mouth turned up on the left side when he smiled, and she looked at his blond wavy hair. "Isn't he cute?" she said.

"Who?" said Eileen.

"Eugene," said Kitty.

"I like the way he talks," said Eileen. " 'Y'all.' He's got a southern drawl. That's cute. I'm going to church."

"I like him," said Kitty.

"What do you mean by that?" demanded

Margaret Mary. "We're too young to get any foolish ideas, my mother says. Those girls are just boy crazy."

"I just mean I like him. Aren't we supposed to like our neighbors? Sister Ursuline says we have to like everyone or we won't go to heaven."

"Oh, well, I like him that way, too," said Margaret Mary. "But not because he's a boy," she added.

The next day Kitty wore her new aqua-colored angora sweater to school, the one she'd received for her birthday. "I need it under my coat," she told her mother. "It's so cold out."

Kitty left it on in school and walked by Eugene's desk, stopping to sharpen a pencil.

"Kitty, would you please put your sweater in the cloakroom. It is not a regulation sweater that can be worn with your uniform."

"Yes, Sister," said Kitty.

At recess she put her sweater back on and said to Margaret Mary and Eileen, "I wonder where that new boy lives . . ."

"Who, Eugene?" said Margaret Mary.

Kitty wondered what other new boy there could be. He was the first new boy in school for ages. "He walks in my line," said Eileen, unwrapping a Hershey bar. "I think he lives over on Niles by Edward Kaiser's house."

"What difference does it make?" said Margaret Mary.

"Just wondered," said Kitty.

"He likes Ruthie," said Eileen, chewing her candy bar.

"Ruthie is boy crazy," said Kitty. "She likes any boy."

"I mean *he* likes *her*," said Eileen.

"Who cares?" said Margaret Mary. "Let's swing."

The next day when they got as far as Jefferson and Margaret Mary went on, Kitty turned around and walked back down Albert Street past school, heading across the field toward Niles Avenue. She began to shiver and pulled up her collar, but although she had a scarf and a cap in her pocket she didn't put them on. She took off her parka hood and fluffed her hair out like Judy Garland's.

When she got to Edward's block, she studied the houses, walking by all of them slowly. Suddenly she saw him coming out one of the back doors. He was taking the garbage out for his mother. "Gene," his mother called, "shovel the sidewalk when you finish." She had a beautiful southern sound in her voice, too.

Kitty hid behind a tree. She hadn't expected this, she had hoped just to see him through a window.

Eugene started to shovel the sidewalk. "Hi," he said.

Kitty looked around. He must be talking to her.

"Y'all got a friend in the neighborhood?"

"I — I'm on my way to Eileen's," said Kitty in a shaky voice. "She lives on Juno."

He leaned on his shovel. "Where y'all live?" he drawled. He didn't have a hat or mittens on and his wavy hair was blowing in the wind. He has beautiful hair, thought Kitty.

"On Jefferson," said Kitty. "One forty-five Jefferson." She brushed snow from her coat. "Do you like Minnesota?"

"It's okay," said Eugene, smiling. He had a nice smile. "Except for the snow. It was warmer in Missouri." Eugene began to shovel again. "See y'all around," he said.

"Yeah, see you around," said Kitty, walking on quickly.

Around the corner she put on her parka hood and tied the scarf around her face. "He likes me!" said Kitty, feeling warm and

cozy inside. "He wants to see me again."

Kitty ran all the way home and told her mother that she had washed blackboards after school. She couldn't go to hell for telling a lie, she decided, when she had a Sacred Heart picture over her bed and had also made the nine First Fridays. Kitty knew that going to mass and communion the first Friday of the month nine times in a row guaranteed heaven. She had heard somewhere that God had appeared in person to a saint and told her so.

The weeks went by and Kitty kept her secret to herself. She thought that any day now Eugene would talk to her again, and maybe he would come by her house because he knew the address. She wore her aqua sweater all the time just in case, even though it shed all over her clothes and anything she got close to.

Valentine's Day was coming and everyone went to the dime store after school to buy

valentines and laugh at the comic ones. Kitty had saved her money and planned to buy Eugene the biggest valentine in the store. She never liked in-between things. She either liked the biggest or the smallest or the best or the worst. She either wanted to win the spelldown or not be in it at all. She hated coming in second in anything. Kitty picked the largest valentine off the rack even though it said, "To the one I love on Valentine's Day." It had a bottle with a ship in it and ducks flying around the edges. It was a man's card, and Eugene was a man, a tall handsome man. Kitty knew she loved him.

She bought other valentines for Eileen and Margaret Mary, ones that said, "My heart pants for You" and "Be Mine," but Eugene's was the only one with a big white envelope. Most of the valentines didn't have white envelopes. Kitty paid for them and went home, wondering if she should sign her name. Of course. She would write it with a red fountain pen. Hardly anyone had red ink.

The next day Father Bauer came into the classroom. After all the children had stood up and said, "Good morning, Father," and asked for his blessing, he said, "I have an announcement. Next week, as you all know, is Valentine's Day." Everyone smiled and nodded their heads. They knew. Father Bauer went on, "Since it was originally a pagan holiday, and has now become so commercial, I have decided that none of the rooms this year will have valentine boxes. The money you would spend on valentines can go for war stamps. We will have a special war stamp drive on February fourteenth in the gymnasium, and God will reward you for thinking of our country."

Eileen raised her hand. "What if we already bought valentines?" she asked.

"Take them back to the store," said Father Bauer.

But Kitty had already signed her valentines and addressed them, so she couldn't take them back. She knew Eileen couldn't take hers back either, and wondered why she'd even asked. Father Bauer was saying, "Sacrifice is the real meaning of freedom. Liberty is at stake and the right to come here to a Catholic school, and to go to church on Sunday."

Valentine's Day arrived, and in the morning the children lined up to go to the gymnasium and buy war stamps. Kitty saw Eugene standing in line next to Ruthie. He was smiling. She had wondered all night what to do with his valentine, thinking that it didn't seem right just to hand it to him. She would have to slip it into his desk somehow.

Sister Regina was playing "Any Bonds Today" and the "White Cliffs of Dover," with her crucifix tapping the piano keys, as the children bought savings stamps to paste in their little books. When the books were filled, they could be turned in for one war bond.

"I'm going to hand out my valentines at recess," whispered Eileen, buying one war stamp.

"I am, too," said Kitty.

"I took mine back," said Margaret Mary. She had bought twenty-five war stamps and pasted them neatly in her book right away. Her stamp book looked neat and straight, like her blouses and her schoolbooks.

At recess, those who had brought valentines passed them out, and everyone hid them in their pockets. Just before the bell rang, Kitty hurried into the room and, looking around to make sure no one was there, slipped Eugene's into his desk. The bell rang a moment later, and everyone came in from recess all rosy and glowing. Sister Ursuline asked them to take out their spellers. But when Kitty opened her desk to take out hers, a white envelope fell out onto her lap. It didn't have a name on it, but it was large, and the flap was sealed. Kitty's heart beat wildly.

She couldn't wait to open it. She stood her speller up on the desk, ripped open the envelope quietly, and pulled out a large red heart edged with with white lace. It was an expensive valentine, she knew. Cupids with bows and arrows were shooting little hearts that said "Love." In the middle, below the shiny red heart, was the word, PLEASE. Inside it said, BE MINE. Kitty looked at the name signed at the bottom in a long careless scrawl. Eugene. The valentine was from Eugene! She could hardly believe it! She looked up and saw him raising his hand because he knew how to spell "oriental." Ruthie was slipping him a note across the aisle.

"It won't do you any good," said Kitty under her breath. "He likes ME!" She had

been right all the time. Eugene did like her. He really truly did.

All afternoon Kitty couldn't think of a thing except the valentine. She memorized everything on it, the words and the pictures and the feel of the lace. She put it back in the envelope to take home with her, then placed it between the pages of her science book so it wouldn't get bent in her book bag. She would take it to bed with her; put it under her pillow. Eugene liked her . . .

She wouldn't tell anyone her secret. It was too important. Yes, she would. She would have to tell Margaret Mary and Eileen. They had to know because now that she would be seeing Eugene after school, she wouldn't be able to play with them as often as she used to. He would probably walk home with her and carry her books and meet her in the morning, and she'd hold on to his arm like Dottie Mergens did with Charles Meader.

Finally the school day was over and the bell rang. Everyone got his wraps on and lined up at the door. When the phonograph started playing "Stars and Stripes Forever," everyone marched out in flanks, down the two broad front staircases. They met in the middle of the first floor hall and marched out the front doors eight abreast.

Outside in the schoolyard, as Kitty was waiting for Margaret Mary and Eileen, she saw Eugene laughing and holding something in his hand. Ruthie and some other girls were giggling and pointing, and she heard Eugene say, "Kitty? Kitty who?"

It was her valentine in his hand. Before they could see her, Kitty ran around the corner of the building. There must be some mistake, she said to herself. She had Eugene's valentine right here inside her science book. It proved he liked her. She must not have heard him right.

"Oh, there you are," said Margaret Mary,

just turning the corner with Eileen. They both had a handful of valentines.

"Hey!" cried Eileen. "I got more valentines this year than last year, when we had a valentine box!"

"I don't think we should take them," said Margaret Mary.

The girls put their book bags down and showed each other their valentines. Margaret Mary and Eileen each had one big one in a white envelope.

"Who is that from?" asked Kitty.

"This?" said Eileen. "It's from that new kid. Pretty, isn't it? He gave every girl in the room one. Isn't it something? Think of all the money that cost. And he bought war stamps, too." Eileen dumped it along with all the others into her book bag.

Margaret Mary was holding one just like it. A red heart with cupids and arrows and the words, "PLEASE. BE MINE." All exactly alike. Every girl in the room, including Delores Henley, was carrying Kitty's card home in her book bag. Kitty felt sick.

She said good-bye to Margaret Mary and Eileen and walked the other way home so that she wouldn't have to go in line. By the time she got to Pascal Street tears were running down her face. When she got home, she ran to her room and, grabbing the valentine out of her book bag, she tore it up into little shreds and threw it away. Then she lay on her bed and cried. She cried and cried until she felt better, and then got up and washed her face and studied her science, and thought, boys are dumb. I'll never ever like any boy again.

6

Finding "Do"

As the days went on, Kitty thought less and less about the valentine and even almost forgot that she had loved Eugene. There were other things to worry about. One was Margaret Mary's news. Sister Ursuline had told her that she had been chosen to crown the statue of the Blessed Virgin with flowers on May Day.

"But that's good news!" said Kitty when Margaret Mary called her. Every girl in the school wanted to wear a long blue dress and carry the wreath of peonies on a satin pillow in the procession to the May altar.

"It would be," said Margaret Mary, "but I don't have a blue dress. I don't have any dress with a high neck and long sleeves that is pretty enough, and my mother says that we can't afford to buy one."

"What will you do?" said Kitty, impatient for a solution.

"My mom said to pray. She said God will find a way and everything will work out."

Kitty doubted the wisdom of that, but Margaret Mary's mother must know. She seemed to know a lot of things.

"Well that's good; then you don't have to worry," said Kitty.

But Margaret Mary did seem to worry, despite what her mother had said.

Kitty had another problem. It was the subject in school that she dreaded most: Music. Not that she couldn't sing. She could. She just couldn't find *do*.

For half a year she had avoided being called on to give the clef reading by staring hard at her music book when Sister Ursuline was scanning the class for someone to call on. If she looked off into space as though she weren't paying attention, Sister was sure to call on her. She always called on people who weren't paying attention. If she looked natural and at ease, as if she knew all about it, Sister might call on her also. Sometimes Sister needed someone who could give a correct answer without wasting time. But Kitty found that if she frowned at the staff in her book as though she were puzzling it out and just needed more time, she'd be fairly safe. Sister would pass her by and call on someone who knew right away, or who wasn't paying attention.

The "teachers" sat in the back row in music class. (Everyone changed seats for music when Sister tapped her pitch pipe on her desk.) The teachers were the students who could stand up and say, "There are three flats in our new song. The right-hand flat is always *fa,* so *do* is on the bottom line and the fourth space."

If you were not a teacher, your chances of being called on were slim. Kitty tried to see to it that she sang poorly so that she would have a front seat like Eileen, who always stared out the window, thinking thoughts far away from music class. She never frowned at the staff or worried about being called on. And she never was.

The best part of the new song was singing the words. But it took so *long* to get to the words. All the notes had to be learned and tapped and sung first. Tap-from-the-wrist-one-two-three-four. Four beats for a whole note, one for a quarter note, one for the rest signs, too. The teacher would advance slowly up each row (Margaret Mary was a teacher) tapping each student on the back and calling off the notes for each line. Kitty hated the whole thing, except for the words. Then they could pick up their books and not have to tap under each note. She liked the review song best of all because they could just sing it. But if the review song went badly, it meant those notes had to be sung too, and the lesson was even more wearying.

One day the review song was "Battle Hymn of the Republic," which was Kitty's favorite. She held her book up high and sang out loud and clear. After it was finished, Sister Ursuline said, "Kitty, you seem to be improving. Would you change places with Gerald please?"

Kitty's stomach suddenly began to ache. Gerald sat in the back row and was a teacher. He knew where *do* was, and the names of all those mysterious sharps and flats. But he had been talking and passing notes, and Sister was Teaching him a Lesson by moving him up front even though he could sing well and knew the scale. Music wasn't everything. Deportment was more important.

Now that Kitty was a target for the clef

reading, her mind raced. Although Margaret Mary had told her over and over how to find *do,* she never understood. Margaret Mary could find *do* in her sleep. Like Jack-be-Nimble, she could rattle off the clef reading on any song. But every note looked the same to Kitty. She looked helplessly across the room to where Eileen was sitting, to see if she could be of any help, but Eileen was still looking out the window.

Slowly Kitty picked up her music book and walked down the aisle to take Gerald's place. He advanced sheepishly to hers. She wanted to call out, "It's all a mistake! I can't sing, AND I SURELY CAN'T READ NOTES!"

"Open your book to the new song, page twenty-four." Sister tapped her pointer at the page number in yellow chalk in the corner of the blackboard. Everyone turned to page 24. Maybe there wouldn't be any sharps or flats, Kitty hoped. She knew the key of C. She prayed, then looked. Four sharps. Kitty prayed for a fire drill.

"Now, who can tell me where *do* is?"

Kitty waved her hand wildly.

"Yes! Kitty!"

"May I be excused to go to the lavatory, Sister?"

Kitty looked at her pleadingly.

Sister frowned. She knew about that excuse, but she was taking a chance if she said no.

"Yes, Kitty."

Kitty closed her book and as she walked toward the door, she heard Sister calling on someone else to find *do*. She went down the hall and into the lavatory and closed the wooden door in the stall and latched it.

"I'll just sit here till music is over," she said to herself.

Classes came in and went out again. A teacher disciplined someone. People splashed water on each other. Girls combed their hair and the eighth graders put on lipstick. Kitty could hear it all. They laughed and kicked the door and said, "Who's in there?" and then went on to joke until a Sister must have appeared, which acted like magic. Quiet came over the girls and there was the soft sound of hands on paper towels, and feet scurrying out the door to get into line.

Everything was silent. Someone should have finished the clef reading by now. In fact, they should be almost finished with the notes of the new song and going on to the words.

Suddenly Kitty heard someone whisper, "Kitty? Kitty? Are you in there?" It was Margaret Mary. "Sister wants to know if you're all right."

"Of course I'm all right."

"Then you better come back to the room."

"I can't find *do*."

"Are you going to sit in here every day?"

"For years."

"That's dumb."

"I'm never coming out. Never never never."

"Then they'll get your mom and dad and there will be a big fuss like when Henry Lees carved with his penknife on his desk."

Kitty thought of her parents being summoned to school because she wouldn't come out of the lavatory. She thought of living there, sleeping there, behind that wooden door with the latch. She could sneak out at night, but by then the school would be locked.

Kitty grew worried. "I wish Eileen were here. She'd know what to do."

"Let's think of what she would do," said Margaret Mary.

Margaret Mary leaned on the washbowl. "I know what she'd say! She'd say, 'So what? When Sister calls on you, just say *do*

97

is on the first line and fourth space, and if it's wrong she'll move you and you probably won't be called on again for at least two months. You'll get your old seat back. That's the worst that could happen.' "

Kitty opened the wooden door. "You sounded just like Eileen!" she said. "That is exactly what she would say. If I do it wrong once, I will get my old place back and Sister won't call on me again because I won't sing well, and I'll frown and look as if I'm thinking hard when it's time for the clef reading."

"You better not sing the review song so well anymore," said Margaret Mary, "or this could happen all over again."

When the girls got back to the room, Eileen was still staring out the window and didn't know about the good advice she'd just given.

The next day Kitty was called on in music and said *do* was on the sixth line (there were only five lines, but Kitty wasn't taking any chances on being right by accident), and the class laughed and Sister changed her seat to the one next to Eileen's. Eileen's advice had been exactly right.

7

The Haunted House

When the worst of the chill was off Saint Paul, the girls grew restless and wanted to be outside after school. Melted snow ran in the gutters, and they walked up Jefferson Avenue with one foot on the street and the other on the curb, straddling the narrow channels of water. If they hadn't been too old, they would have liked to sail boats down these alleys.

"It stays light longer now," said Kitty to Eileen, who was walking her halfway home, as far as the old house. The girls were carrying their teddy bear coats and took off their parkas as well. "Pretty soon we can wear anklets instead of these long stockings."

"I hate garter belts," said Eileen, looking down at her long white stockings. She was the only one who wore white ones. And they never had holes in them, or darns. Her mother just kept buying her new ones. All the other girls wore brown stockings to school.

The girls sat down on the steps of the old house. They wrote KILROY WAS HERE on their notebooks and drew him with his nose hanging over the edge of a wall. They drew hearts and arrows and Nazi signs and American flags. Eileen was busy writing along the edges of the closed pages of her science book: "In case of fire, throw in."

"You are defacing a book," said Kitty. "That's what Sister Ursuline calls it."

Eileen went on printing laboriously, over and over with her lead pencil until it was good and dark.

Kitty stared up at the old house. "I'd love to go inside," she said.

"It's haunted," said Eileen dreamily.

"I'd go in anyway," said Kitty, shivering at the thought. "It's so big and old and scary. I wonder if there really are children imprisoned up in that tower, starving to death."

The girls stared at the house.

"Did you see something move in that upstairs window?" asked Eileen.

"No," said Kitty. "But it could have just been someone who lives there."

"It was a ghost," said Eileen casually.

"A ghost?" said Kitty. "How do you know it was a ghost?"

"I've seen ghosts."

The girls knew that Eileen had seen ghosts. One night, she had told them once, she saw one in her bedroom. It had moved in slowly from the doorway and hovered over her bed. She had been positive it was a ghost and everyone had believed her because she had crossed her heart and hoped to die if it wasn't a ghost. No one ever thought to doubt her. If Eileen said it was a ghost, it was a ghost.

"Was it all white?"

"No silly, ghosts aren't white. They are kind of shapeless things like air, only you can see that they are there. They don't actually have bodies, you know."

"Like angels? Just their spirit?"

Eileen wasn't too fond of angels. "Like ghosts," she said. "I want to see the inside of that house."

Kitty shivered. "It would be fun. I wish we knew who lived there. What if it were a place where we could baby-sit?"

"Ghosts don't have babies," said Eileen, tossing her head and making her curls spin. "Somebody old must live there who walks with a bent stick, probably, and has a pointed chin." She stood up. "Well, I'm going to see."

"Eileen, what are you going to do, just walk in and say 'let me see your ghost'?"

Eileen thought for a moment. "No, we have to have a reason for being there. If we don't know the people we have to be either a priest or a salesman to get in somebody's house." Eileen toyed with the idea of being a priest, but she discarded it quickly when she realized that she wouldn't look anything like Father Bauer, even with a black suit on.

"What could we sell?" she said. The girls looked down at their pile of clothes and books. Eileen's glance fell on Kitty's pencil case.

"Pencils!" she said. "That would work, but what we need is more than one — and they have to look alike. No one would go selling all different kinds of pencils. Let's see yours."

Kitty could feel goose bumps on her skin. This was getting scary. Still, it wasn't wrong to be a salesman. "Eileen," she said quivering, "we could get in all kinds of houses this way!"

Eileen had already thought of that. "If we have enough pencils that match," she said. "And if no one buys too many."

Kitty unzipped her pencil case. She took out one red Coca-Cola pencil and one shorter one that was chewed and had UNCLE SAM WANTS YOU printed along its side.

"Nothing else?" said Eileen.

Kitty shook her head.

Eileen picked up the pencil she had been defacing her book with. "This is a Coca Cola pencil too," she said. "That makes two alike. That's enough."

Kitty put Uncle Sam away and zipped her pencil case. "Should we practice on a smaller house first?" she asked.

"That would be silly," said Eileen. "They might buy our pencils, and then we wouldn't have two alike to take to the haunted house." Eileen was always very reasonable. Kitty wondered why she hadn't thought of that.

The girls put on their coats and picked up their things. The sun was getting lower and lower in the west, and strange shadows had begun to fall over the large house. The setting sun made the panes of glass shine golden and rose, even though they were covered with cobwebs.

"Maybe we should wait till tomorrow," said Kitty.

"Why?" asked Eileen. "We're here now."

They walked up the steps and along the overgrown path, and as they got closer the house looked different. The screen on the door was rusty, as though it had been on for many winters. Kitty wanted to turn around and run, but before she could, Eileen went up to the door quickly and knocked. She seemed impatient, as if the ghost inside had no business keeping her waiting. She knocked again. The girls heard footsteps moving inside. Then a woman's face peered out a crack in the door.

"Yes?" she said.

"We are selling pencils," said Eileen.

"Whatever for?" asked the woman.

Eileen could think quickly. "Charity," she said.

The woman smiled and opened the door. "Come in," she said.

Eileen had been right! It did work! They were inside the house!

"How much are your pencils?"

"A penny each," said Eileen.

"Fine, I can use ten," she said. "I'm always looking for a pencil around here."

"We only have two left," said Eileen.

"We could bring you more tomorrow," said Kitty hopefully.

The woman smiled again, a wide, friendly smile. "Two will be fine," she said. "I'll get you a nickel. Come and sit down, won't you?"

The girls walked over to a mohair couch and sat down, looking around slowly.

"Wow!" said Kitty, after the woman had left. "This looks like a castle. Look at the winding stairs. And the mirrors."

On one wall was a bookcase, and magazines and books lay scattered about the room as though someone had just put them down. But what they noticed most of all were the canaries singing. Everywhere they looked were canary cages, on tables, on radiators, on sofas, hanging from stands and brackets and poles.

"Here we are!" said the woman, returning with a nickel. "Keep the change." Eileen handed her the pencils and thanked her.

"My name is Charlotte Neilson. What are yours?"

Charlotte sat down in a chair with two lions' heads carved on the back and crossed her legs. She lit a cigarette in a long silver holder and tapped it every so often in a brass ashtray that stood beside the chair.

She had on a blue velvet dress and diamond earrings and silk stockings, even though it was only four o'clock in the afternoon. Her brown hair was coming out of its chignon and fell in wisps about her ears, and her slip hung a bit below her dress. One stocking had a run in it. She seemed out of breath and excited, and after the girls introduced themselves, she said, "Won't you stay for supper? I have some oxtail soup cooking in the basement. Would you like a bowl of hot soup?"

Eileen was just about to say yes when Kitty said in a louder voice, "I think our mothers would worry, Mrs. Neilson. It's getting dark."

"Not Mrs.," she said, smiling. "Miss. Of course they'd worry. It is nice to have visitors, though. You must come back when you can stay awhile."

"Really?" said Kitty.

"Of course," said Charlotte Neilson. "I

live alone here — well, except for my nine canaries." She waved her hand in a sweeping gesture that included all the cages. "I would like a cat, but then of course that wouldn't be practical."

"We like your house," said Kitty in a friendly burst of confidence.

Charlotte laughed a tinkling laugh like tinsel on a Christmas tree. "It's too big to take care of," she said. "It was my grandmother's house and has been in the family for years, you know. But I'm the only one left now. My birds and I."

It was quiet except for the piercing songs of the canaries. Then a clock chimed in one of the rooms, and there was a sound like wind in a chimney or fireplace.

She stood up. "Why don't you come back some afternoon, and I will show you the rest of the house."

"We'd like that!" said Kitty.

"You just tell your mothers you are going

to the old Neilson house. They'll know."

The girls picked up their things and thanked Miss Neilson. She let them out the front door and blew them a kiss. "Come again!" she called.

"We will," they replied.

Miss Neilson watched the girls go down the winding walk. "Pencils!" she said to herself and smiled. "Pencils!" she said again and bent over, rocking with laughter.

"Eileen!" said Kitty. "She is no ghost! There's no ghost in that house. And she doesn't have a pointed chin and walk with a bent stick! I think she's a queen. She looks regal, and queens wear velvet in the daytime. And diamonds. She is a queen, Eileen!"

"She's probably not a ghost," Eileen admitted. "But she might be a witch. She has a high voice, and her hair looks kind of witchlike. And she wears old silk stockings

with runs in them. Upstairs might be a dungeon where she keeps little kids she lures into her house. Did you ever hear of oxtail soup? I wonder what else is in it. I'll bet it's a cauldron that's bubbling all the time and she probably throws the kids she steals into it."

"Eileen! She's a queen, I know she's a queen. And I think we should put the nickel she gave us in the poor box at church. You go right by on the way home, why don't you drop it in?"

"I s'pose," said Eileen, starting down the street. "See you tomorrow."

Kitty waved and hurried toward Jefferson Avenue. Her dad would be coming from the streetcar line. She couldn't wait to tell him that there might be a queen living in Saint Paul. And only four blocks away!

8

Inside Looking Out

Kitty not only told her father and mother about Miss Neilson (the girls couldn't seem to call her "Charlotte") but she quickly called Margaret Mary to tell her about going inside the old house. Margaret Mary was worrying in earnest now about her blue dress for May Day (May was very close), but she agreed to join Kitty and Eileen for a visit to Miss Neilson's the following afternoon.

The next day right after school, the three girls walked up the steps and along the path to Miss Neilson's front door.

"This time it doesn't feel scary at all coming here," said Kitty leading the way. She knocked at the door. In a few moments it flew open, and Miss Neilson stood with her arms thrown out to welcome them.

"You have come to see me again," she said, opening the screen door. She was wearing the same velvet dress and was holding her silver cigarette holder between two fingers.

"This is our friend, Margaret Mary," said Kitty.

Margaret Mary smiled and held out her hand, but Miss Neilson put her arms around her and hugged her and said, "Why, any friend of Kitty and Eileen's is my friend, too. Come in girls, come in. You have come to see me, what a lovely surprise. And this time you are not selling pencils." She laughed.

"We sold them all," said Eileen.

"And we gave the money to the poor," added Kitty, feeling a bit guilty, although she hadn't really told a lie.

The girls sat on the mohair couch as they had yesterday. And like the day before, the canaries were singing in high, piercing voices.

"Now!" said Miss Neilson. "What can I get you? I know! A tea party, that's what we will have, a tea party." She walked through a doorway into a hall that led to the kitchen, and the girls could hear her putting a kettle of water on the stove. "Jasmine tea," she called. "We will have jasmine tea, and some biscuits with honey. Do you like jasmine tea?" she called.

"Yes," called Eileen, "I love jasmine tea, Miss Neilson."

The girls looked at her. Margaret Mary and Kitty had never heard of jasmine tea.

"Good," called Miss Neilson, coming back into the room.

"You see this little bell," she said, pointing to a small black button over the mohair couch. "We used to press it for the maid, and she would bring the tea and then I

117

didn't have to run back and forth." She pressed it and a buzzing noise could be heard out in the kitchen. "But now of course, there is just me, and I don't need a maid." She smiled. "While we are waiting for the water to boil, let me show you my house."

Those were the words the girls had waited so long to hear!

Miss Neilson led the girls through two large doors leading out of the living room and said, "This was my father's library." The girls looked at the rows of dusty leather books that lined the shelves along the walls. There was a fireplace in here, too, and a desk in the corner.

"Oh, a window seat!" said Margaret Mary, running over to a bay window with a cushioned seat beneath it.

"That is where I used to sit and read on long winter afternoons when I was your age," said Miss Neilson. "My father was a

doctor and all these old medical books be-
longed to him," she waved her hand in the
direction of the book shelves. "But I sat in
the window seat and read all about Ethel
Barrymore and dreamed of becoming an
actress," she said.

Miss Neilson swept out of the room, and
the girls followed behind the scent of Evening in Paris perfume.

"Didn't I tell you she was a queen?" whispered Kitty to Margaret Mary.

"She's beautiful," said Margaret Mary.

"We'll have our tea before we go upstairs," said Miss Neilson. "Sit here at the
table," she said, pushing magazines aside.
"I'll be right in."

In a moment Miss Neilson came in,
wheeling a wicker teacart with a silver tea-
pot and four china plates and cups and sau-
cers. She placed a cup and plate before
each of the girls, along with a silver napkin
ring encircling a linen napkin. Then she

put a china sugar bowl and creamer with small blue violets painted on them in the middle of the table.

"Now," she said, pouring the tea, "have a biscuit and honey. And here are some grapes and cheese. Help yourself."

The girls watched Miss Neilson. She spread the linen napkin on her lap and they did the same, The fragrance of jasmine flowers floated in the air, and Kitty thought she must be dreaming. Maybe she was a storybook princess and this wasn't happening at all.

Kitty and Margaret Mary each put four lamps of sugar in their tea and sipped it slowly. Eileen drank hers with no sugar or cream and held her cup the way Miss Neilson did, with her little finger out, as if she drank jasmine tea every day.

"Did you become an actress?" asked Eileen suddenly, remembering Miss Neilson's dream.

"Yes," she said. "As a matter of fact I did. I was on the stage in Saint Paul and Minneapolis with the Twin City Drama Company, and then I went to Chicago."

"Chicago!" said Margaret Mary. "My uncle went to Chicago for the World's Fair, and he brought me a souvenir."

"Well, I did some acting in Chicago with a theater group there. Then we went on tour, and then," she said, tapping her cigarette in a glass ashtray with pink cupids on the sides, "I became engaged to be married to a man I acted with."

The girls stared at Miss Neilson and waited for her to continue. She blew a long puff of blue smoke up over her head and was quiet.

"Yes?" said Kitty. "Did you marry him?"

"Did you go on acting?" asked Eileen.

"Did you give up acting and have a big wedding with a long white dress?" asked Margaret Mary.

Miss Neilson laughed her light, tinkling laugh. "No," she said, "I didn't marry and I had to give up the stage."

Margaret Mary felt tears forming in the corners of her eyes. Eileen frowned.

"Why?" asked Kitty.

"My father died, and I came home to take care of my mother," Miss Neilson replied after a moment. "She was all alone here and she needed me."

Eileen was angry. "I would have stayed in Chicago and been an actress," she said.

Kitty and Margaret Mary looked at her disapprovingly. "And leave her poor mother all alone?" said Kitty.

"Her mother could have come to Chicago," said Eileen.

Miss Neilson smiled. "By that time my mother was too ill to travel, and she was too old to move to a new city. So! I packed up my things and came back to Saint Paul. But now. I must show you the house! You must see the turrets!" She stood up and waved the hand with the diamonds toward the winding staircase. It was long and wide and wooden, with carvings of lions' heads on the posts just like the ones that decorated the back of the chair she had been sitting on. "Follow me!" she called.

The girls walked up the steps behind Miss Neilson. When they got to the landing they looked down. They could see the room below and the stained-glass window with the sun coming through it. The canaries were shrilling and the clock was chiming the hour.

"I feel as if I'm in a movie," said Kitty.

"Like *Gone with the Wind*," said Eileen, who loved Scarlett O'Hara.

Miss Neilson was way above them by now. "Come on, girls!" she called, leaning over the banister and looking down at them. "It's three floors up to the tower rooms."

"Tower rooms! Towers are in castles!" said Kitty. "We're in a castle!" They rushed up the rest of the way.

"Here we are," said Miss Neilson. "This is my tower! I hardly ever come up here, so it's a bit dusty," she said, wiping her finger across a window ledge and tapping her cigarette in a vase that stood on a small table.

The girls looked out the windows, down to the steps where they'd sat so often, wondering about this very tower, dreaming of orphans and dungeons and ghosts. And here they were. Really inside. They could see over the treetops as far as Saint Anthony's, and almost as far as Jefferson Avenue. They were inside at last, looking out.

"This is what I have to show you," said Miss Neilson. The girls turned from the window and looked around to where she was standing. Along one side of the tower wall was a rack hung with dresses. Dresses of velvet and sequins; and veils and capes.

Dresses with hoops and pleats and sashes and bustles. All covered with cellophane wrap to protect them.

"My dresses," she said. "Some of them are costumes from plays that I was in. My mother and I made most of them," she added. "And in these trunks," the girls eyes followed Miss Neilson as she knelt on the floor and threw open the covers of several large dusty trunks, "are all my hats and shoes."

Flowery hats and high-heeled, open-toed shoes tumbled out of the trunks as she struggled to reach the bottom of one and lifted out a yellowed white satin gown with a veil wrapped in tissue paper. "This would have been my wedding dress," she said cheerfully.

Margaret Mary began to sniff, but Eileen, ignoring the others, was holding the dresses up to her one at a time and looking at her reflection in the window.

"Now!" said Charlotte Neilson. "Let's try them on! Choose any you like and we'll pin them up at the waist to make them fit."

"Really?" said Kitty. It seemed too good to be true.

"Of course," said Miss Neilson.

Eileen was already pulling a yellow organdy dress over her head, one with a large hoop and wide ruffle around the hem. The top fell in ruffles from the shoulder.

"You look just like Scarlett O'Hara," shouted Margaret Mary.

Miss Neilson stepped back and frowned. "We have to take it in a bit, and redo your hair," she said. She ran downstairs and came back a short time later with clothespins, which she clipped to the back of the dress to take it in, and a comb and powder and make-up. She parted Eileen's hair in the middle and combed it in front of her ears. Then she went through a trunk and found a large, yellow straw hat with a wide brim and streamers down the back. "Put it on," she said.

"Eileen," said Kitty breathlessly, "you look beautiful!"

Kitty was trying on a shorter one with ruffles, which looked like a dance dress. She had always wanted to dance like Ginger Rogers, and this was exactly the dress for it.

All of a sudden, Margaret Mary called, "Look!" The girls turned around to see Margaret Mary standing in a long blue taffeta dress with long sleeves and a high neck with lace around it. Small pearl buttons ran from the collar to the waist, and the skirt stood out around her in a circle.

"The Blessed Virgin!" said Kitty. "You look like the Blessed Virgin, Margaret Mary!"

"No, she looks like she could crown the Blessed Virgin in that dress," said Eileen thoughtfully. Kitty explained to Miss Neilson about Margaret Mary's being chosen for May Day and not having a dress.

"How good you came today," said Miss Neilson. "Now you have a dress, and it only needs to be taken in at the waist and shortened a bit," she said, checking the fit. "Can your mother take in the seams, dear?" She felt the material between her fingers. "It is in fine condition; it will just need a good pressing."

Margaret Mary looked at Miss Neilson. "Do you mean I can wear it in the May procession?" she said softly.

"Why, of course, my dear. Whyever not?" She hugged Margaret Mary. "How fine that the dress will be of use again. All these lovely things and no one to wear them!"

Margaret Mary looked as if she might cry again. Kitty had tears in her eyes, too. Margaret Mary's mother had been right, she realized, when she told her not to worry about having a blue dress in time for May Day.

Eileen broke the spell. "If you *have* to crown the Blessed Virgin, that is just the dress to do it in."

"Now," said Miss Neilson, "your mothers will be worried. We must pack up the dress in a box, and you will come back another day and try the other things on and maybe put on a little play."

Kitty's head swam with all she was hearing. And to think that they had once believed Miss Neilson's house was haunted.

The girls hugged Miss Neilson before they left and thanked her and asked if they could come back soon. She told them that she played bingo on Wednesdays and folded bandages for the Red Cross on Fridays, but that they could come any other day. Then she blew them a kiss, and closed the door.

"And you thought she was a witch," said Kitty to Eileen.

"Well, she isn't a queen."

"She's an actress," said Kitty, "and that's even better."

"She's a saint, that's what she is," said Margaret Mary, hugging the box with the dress in it to her chest. "My mother told me to pray and not to worry and she was right."

"Well I think it was luck," said Eileen, skipping along the sidewalk. "We were lucky Miss Neilson had a blue dress."

Margaret Mary and Kitty frowned. They didn't believe in luck. They both knew Margaret Mary's mother was right; God had taken care of it.

On May Day, Margaret Mary crowned the Blessed Virgin and Kitty cried because Margaret Mary looked so beautiful. Everyone walked in the procession and when they sang the line, "From gay and verdant bow-ow'rs, we haste to-oo crown thee-ee now," Margaret Mary placed the wreath of peonies on Mary's head. It was a wonderful day.

The girls went back often to visit Miss Neilson, and before long it was summer and school was out.

On the last day, Father Bauer said the mass that officially closed the school year. He turned to the students and sang, *"EEE-TAY, MEE-SA EST"* for the last time. The altar boys responded, *"DAY-OOH GRAATS-EE-AS!"* The mass was over. Thanks be to God.

The girls walked out of church into the bright sunlight and thought about summer.

"I'll be going to Norwood to stay with my Aunt Katie," said Kitty. Kitty's aunt worked in the church in Norwood, cleaning the altar and ironing the priest's vestments and scraping the wax off the vigil light holders. "I'll get to ring the Angelus. I love to ring the church bell. You pull this long rope and everyone even out in the country can hear it."

"I'm going to Scituate again," said Eileen. She went to Scituate, Massachusetts, every summer. It was near Boston, and last year she had sent back pictures of herself swimming in the ocean and standing next to Plymouth Rock and in front of Paul Revere's house. "I'm going to see Louisa May Alcott's house this year," she added.

"Really?" said Kitty. "Her real house?"

"Of course, why would I see one that wasn't real?" said Eileen, biting into the apple from her lunch. "It's where she wrote *Little Women*. We're going to go through it and see her bedroom and where she wrote and everything."

The girls looked at Eileen with admiration. They had never been outside Minnesota.

"I'll send you picture postcards from wherever we go," Eileen assured them.

"Are you going anywhere, Margaret Mary?" asked Kitty.

"I'll be home taking care of my little

brother," she said. "My mother says I have all my life to travel, and anyway I have to help her can peaches and pick strawberries and clean cupboards and mend clothes. She says someday I'll thank her because I'll know so much about housekeeping."

Margaret Mary did know a lot about housekeeping. She was definitely the only one of the girls who could cook a meal or iron a shirt. Kitty's mother never let her in the kitchen because she said she made a mess and didn't clean up.

"I think it's sad," said Kitty, looking as though she might cry. "We won't see each other every day anymore and we'll go away and maybe forget all about each other for-ever."

Eileen chewed her apple. "How could we," she said. "In September we will be right back here in fifth grade, looking at Sister Magdelene's ugly face instead of Sister Ursuline's." She threw her apple core into the bridal wreath bushes.

"Eileen, it's a sin to call nuns ugly. Or anyone ugly."

"They *are* ugly," said Eileen. "If they smiled I bet they'd crack their faces."

"You'll both be back before long," said Margaret Mary, changing the subject, "and we'll be going to Miss Neilson's again. Aren't we lucky to have each other for friends? We should thank God every day for good friends, my mother says."

Kitty started to cry in earnest.

Eileen put her arm around her suddenly and said, "I'll call you both the minute I get home."

Margaret Mary and Kitty started down Albert Street, waving good-bye as they went. Eileen turned and walked away across the field toward Juno Avenue with her curls bouncing.

MS READ-a-thon— a simple way to start youngsters reading

Boys and girls between 6 and 14 can join the MS READ-a-thon and help find a cure for Multiple Sclerosis by reading books. And they get two rewards — the enjoyment of reading, and the great feeling that comes from helping others.

Parents and educators: For complete information call your local MS chapter. Or mail the coupon below.

Kids can help, too!

- - - - - - - - - - - - - - - -

Mail to:
National Multiple Sclerosis Society
205 East 42nd Street
New York, N.Y. 10017

I would like more information about the MS READ-a-thon and how it can work in my area.

Name_____
(please print)

Address_____

City_____ State_____ Zip_____

Organization_____

1—80